AFRICA

ANNETTE WHIPPLE

Rourke
Educational Media

rourkeeducationalmedia.com

Before & After Reading Activities

Before Reading:

Building Academic Vocabulary and Background Knowledge

Before reading a book, it is important to tap into what your child or students already know about the topic. This will help them develop their vocabulary, increase their reading comprehension, and make connections across the curriculum.

1. *Look at the cover of the book. What will this book be about?*
2. *What do you already know about the topic?*
3. *Let's study the Table of Contents. What will you learn about in the book's chapters?*
4. *What would you like to learn about this topic? Do you think you might learn about it from this book? Why or why not?*
5. *Use a reading journal to write about your knowledge of this topic. Record what you already know about the topic and what you hope to learn about the topic.*
6. *Read the book.*
7. *In your reading journal, record what you learned about the topic and your response to the book.*
8. *After reading the book complete the activities below.*

Content Area Vocabulary

Read the list. What do these words mean?

archeologists
colonies
dormant
enslaved
industry
mosaic
natural resources
primates
rural
safari
urban

After Reading:

Comprehension and Extension Activity

After reading the book, work on the following questions with your child or students in order to check their level of reading comprehension and content mastery.

1. What are some examples of the variety in Africa? (Summarize)
2. Why are there so many endemic species on Madagascar? (Infer)
3. Why did European countries build colonies in Africa? (Asking Questions)
4. How does Africa compare to where you live? (Text to Self Connection)
5. What challenges do the people of Africa face? (Asking Questions)

Extension Activity

Compare a population map and a physical map of Africa. Where do the fewest people live? Where do the most people live? Are there cities in the deserts? What types of landforms are cities built close to? If possible, use Google Earth to explore Africa's geography and special features.

TABLE OF CONTENTS

Countries in Africa:

- Algeria
- Angola
- Benin
- Botswana
- Burkina Faso
- Burundi
- Cameroon
- Cape Verde
- Central African Republic (CAR)
- Chad
- Comoros
- Democratic Republic of the Congo
- Cote d'Ivoire
- Djibouti
- Egypt
- Equatorial Guinea
- Eritrea
- Ethiopia
- Gabon
- Gambia
- Ghana
- Guinea
- Guinea-Bissau
- Kenya
- Lesotho
- Liberia
- Libya
- Madagascar
- Malawi
- Mali
- Mauritania
- Mauritius
- Morocco
- Mozambique
- Namibia
- Niger
- Nigeria
- Rwanda
- Sao Tome and Principe
- Republic of the
- Congo
- Senegal
- Seychelles
- Sierra Leone
- Somalia
- South Africa
- South Sudan
- Sudan
- Swaziland
- Tanzania
- Togo
- Tunisia
- Uganda
- Zambia
- Zimbabwe

WELCOME TO AFRICA

When you think of Africa, do you think of wild lions or big deserts? You'll find both on the world's second-largest continent. But they are just two parts of Africa.

Africa is a land of many nations, languages, and cultures. Small villages and savannas are plentiful, but so are modern cities, deserts, and rain forests. Africa even has snow-capped mountains.

Africa's Fast Facts

Land area: 11,724,000 square miles (30,365,021 square kilometers)
Population: 1.26 billion people
Three most common languages: Swahili, French, and English
Number of countries: 54
Largest country: Algeria
Smallest country: Seychelles
Largest cities: Lagos, Nigeria and Cairo, Egypt

Some people think Africa is a country. But it's a continent. It contains 54 countries. That's more than any other continent!

To understand Africa, think of it like a **mosaic**. The land, climate, wildlife, history, and people fit together to make a picture. The finished mosaic is a picture of Africa. It's made of thousands of pieces.

Africa takes up about one-fifth of Earth's land. What does the land look like? It depends on where you are.

Grasslands called savannas blanket about half of Africa. Savannas have rainy and dry seasons. Elephants, lions, and giraffes make their homes in a famous savanna called the Serengeti Plains.

On the Serengeti Plains, a zebra joins a herd of blue wildebeests during their migration.

Deserts receive little rainfall during the year. Africa has many hot deserts.

The Sahara is a huge desert. It is about the same size as the contiguous United States!

Giant sand dunes called *ergs* stretch for miles across the Sahara. Ergs cover large parts of Algeria and Libya. They can reach over 1,000 feet (304 meters) high. That's as tall as a 100-story skyscraper.

Not all of the land is dry. Africa's tropical rain forests are warm and humid. More than 13 feet (4 meters) of rain falls there every year. Like other jungles, the rain forests are home to many plants and animals.

The 20 million people who live near Lake Chad depend on it for irrigation, drinking water, and fish. But it has been overused. Lake Chad is shrinking! It was about 15,500 square miles (40,145 square kilometers) in size. It shrunk to about 300 square miles (777 square kilometers) in just 40 years.

The Ethiopian Highlands and Atlas Mountains are in Africa's mountainous regions. Mount Kilimanjaro is a **dormant** volcano. It's close to the equator, but it's so tall that snow covers it all year long!

The Nile River begins in Lake Victoria. It flows north through ten countries and the Sahara. It empties into the Mediterranean Sea. At 4,132 miles (6,650 kilometers) in length, it is the world's longest river. Millions of people live along the Nile River.

WILD AFRICA

Many species of plants and animals live throughout Africa.

The "Big Five" mammals live in the grasslands. These are elephants, lions, leopards, rhinoceroses, and Cape buffalo. Many visitors go on **safari** to see the amazing animals.

Lots of other animals live in Africa, too. The rain forests are home to many of the world's **primates**. More than 2,000 species of birds live in Africa. Even penguins call this continent home.

About 10,000 kinds of plants live in the Congo Basin's huge rain forest. More than 1,000 plants are unique to the region. They're called endemic species. That means they cannot be found anywhere else in the world.

The roots of Congo rain forest trees are shallow so they can absorb more water from the soil.

About two million wildebeest, zebras, and gazelles migrate in Tanzania and Kenya. The animals travel more than 1,000 miles (1,600 kilometers) searching for feeding grounds and clean water.

The island of Madagascar is located off the southeastern coast of Africa. About 75 percent of Madagascar's plants and animals are found only on this island and nowhere else. Lemurs, tomato frogs, and the Madagascar long-eared owl are a few of its unique species. Unfortunately, many species found on the island are threatened or endangered.

Africa's Wild World Records

Longest river in the world: Nile River
Largest tropical lake in the world: Lake Victoria
Largest hot desert in the world: Sahara
Hottest desert in the world: Sahara
Largest land mammal in the world: African elephant
Smallest land mammal in the world: Etruscan pygmy shrew
Largest bird in the world: ostrich

Etruscan pygmy shrew

Lake Victoria

Ostrich

African elephant

A Long History

Africa has a long history. Scientists think the first humans lived in Africa.

Ancient Egypt might be the most famous old civilization in Africa. The ancient Egyptians built pyramids and temples. Historians, **archeologists**, and tourists still visit the ruins. They want to learn more about the past.

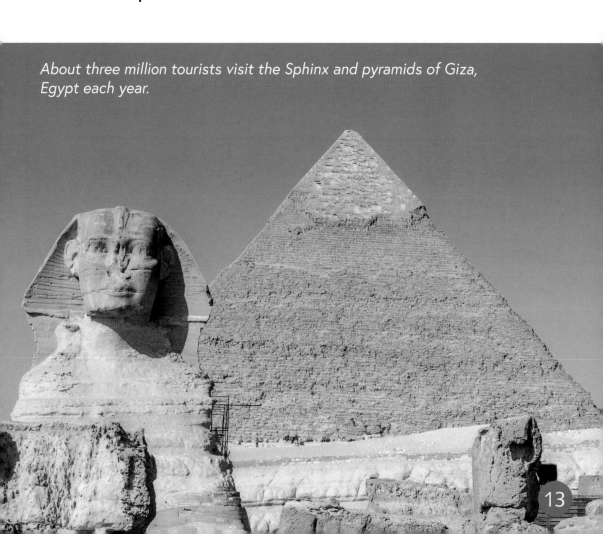

About three million tourists visit the Sphinx and pyramids of Giza, Egypt each year.

Europeans began to explore Africa's coastlines in the 1400s. Later they went farther inland. Europeans were interested in trading items for ivory, spices, and gold. They built forts and castles to hold their goods.

Ivory from elephants was in high demand in Europe and later America for items such as piano keys and knife handles.

The Cape Coast Castle was one of about 60 fortresses and castles built for the gold trade along Ghana's coast. Later, these castles were used as prisons. The prisoners had little food and no toilets. They couldn't leave the dungeons until they were taken to the Americas as slaves.

Portugal and other countries found another way to make money. They wanted to sell Africans as slaves. Slave traders kidnapped Africans from their homes and villages.

Once captured, the slaves were chained on ships. Possibly more than 10 million **enslaved** Africans were sent to North and South America. They were sold there.

Slave traders took European goods to Africa. These items were exchanged for African slaves.

People in the Americas bought slaves instead of paying workers. The slaves had to do hard work. The owners treated them poorly. The slaves were separated from their families forever.

An overseer watches slaves pick cotton on a Louisiana plantation in the 1800s.

Ancient Timbuktu

Goods from western Africa, northern Africa, and beyond were traded in Timbuktu, Mali. By the 13th century, people traveled there to trade gold and salt. Ivory, kola nuts, and books were also exchanged. Merchants and scholars moved to Timbuktu. The city became a business, educational, and spiritual center.

COLONIZATION OF AFRICA

Europeans focused on Africa's land in the 1800s. This time in history became known as the "scramble for Africa." The European countries competed for land control.

Four hundred years of slave trade made communities weak in Africa. Europeans wanted Africa's land and **natural resources**, especially gold and diamonds. Great Britain, France, and other European countries took over almost all of the continent. They built **colonies**.

Powerful European countries came together for the Congo Conference of 1884 - 1885 in Berlin to negotiate their claims of African territories. African people did not have a say at the conference.

Colonization changed Africa. New colonies and new borders were created. Europeans moved to Africa. They brought smallpox, a deadly disease.

Africa has more than 3,000 ethnic groups. Ethnic groups share languages, practices, and ideas unique to their group. The groups were divided and mixed during colonization. European officials encouraged conflict between groups. That way the European countries could stay in power.

Deep conflicts and violence are still common because of race and ethnic tensions.

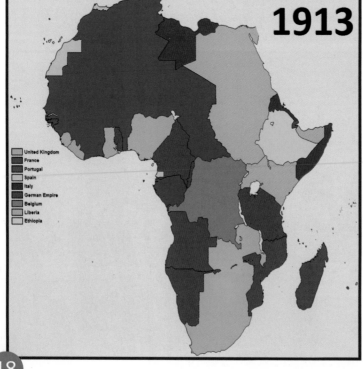

1913

Legend:
- United Kingdom
- France
- Portugal
- Spain
- Italy
- German Empire
- Belgium
- Liberia
- Ethiopia

Almost all of Africa was colonized by European countries during the "scramble for Africa."

Africa's Challenges

Only three countries in Africa had their own government in 1950. Over time, all the nations gained independence. Some countries became free peacefully. Others fought for it.

Independence didn't solve all their problems. Many African countries have corrupt rulers. They make choices that are not good for the people.

Congolese people protested in London because of the British government's involvement with the Democratic Republic of the Congo.

Less than five percent of Africans have access to landline telephones. Cell phones are commonly used for talking, texting, and taking photos and videos. Mobile Money, called M-Pesa, is an easy way to transfer money between two people using cell phones. This service began in Kenya.

Health and poverty are major concerns. In parts of Africa, garbage and bathroom waste are not disposed of properly. This leads to unsafe drinking water and dangerous conditions. People also die from diseases such as malaria and HIV/AIDS. Proper waste control and clean water are needed.

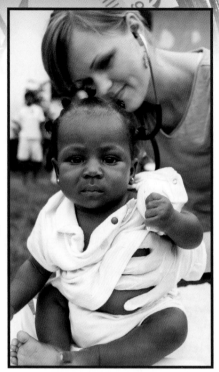

Changes are happening in health care. More nurses, doctors, and health workers are being trained. Telemedicine connects patients in remote areas with doctors using cameras and phones or computers.

A child in Africa dies from malaria every 30 seconds. This disease is spread by mosquitoes. Treatment can be hard to find. It is even harder for people to pay for medical care. Special nets help prevent the spread of malaria, but it's still a problem.

Attending school isn't easy for many African children. In some areas, there are no schools. In some places, families must pay for education, uniforms, and books. The costs often prevent girls and orphans from going to school, and some children must work instead of studying.

Progress is being made, though. More children, especially girls, are staying in school. When the children grow up, they help others. Knowledge leads to change.

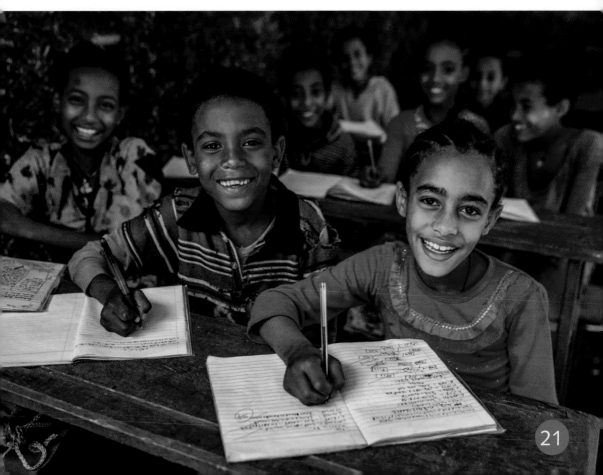

AFRICA'S PEOPLE

Africa is the second-most populated continent. More than a billion people live there. They speak more than 1,500 languages.

More than half of Africans live in small villages and **rural** areas. For centuries, many lived in mud-and-thatch huts. These huts are still common. For many, farming and herding are a way of life. Some grow only what their family needs. Others sell their crops.

Mud-and-thatch huts make up the buildings in this traditional Konso Ethiopian village.

Many people are moving to cities for a different life. Some **urban** residents live in modern apartments. Adults might work in skyscrapers. Families shop in grocery stores and visit parks and movie theaters.

More than 51 million trees were planted to prevent erosion and provide firewood as part of the Green Belt Movement. The project created jobs for poor women. Wangari Maathai, from Kenya, was the first African woman to earn the Nobel Peace Prize in 2004 for her work with the Green Belt Movement.

The creative arts are a growing and major business in Africa. Music has always been an important part of African culture. Nigeria's film **industry**, called Nollywood, makes more movies each year than Hollywood. Senegal is famous for its artists and handmade crafts. South Africa has a strong influence in the worldwide fashion industry.

Mining is strong in Africa. In the Democratic Republic of the Congo, miners dig for cobalt and other minerals. They are sold to make lithium-ion batteries. The batteries make smartphone, laptop, and electric car technology possible. Many miners, including children, work long hours in unsafe conditions for little pay.

Soccer is a much-loved sport throughout the continent. 2010 FIFA World Cup was held in South Africa.

African children love to play. Games are especially popular. Hand-clapping games, jump rope, and hide-and-seek are common. Kids delight in watching movies and playing video games. Football—known as soccer in the United States—is incredibly popular.

ACTIVITY: MANCALA

Many versions of the mancala game exist because it has been played for many centuries. Mancala likely began in Africa and is still a popular game today. Mancala can be played in a variety of ways. This "seeds and holes" game can even be played in the dirt or online! Here's how you can make your own mancala game.

Supplies:
- egg carton, with lid removed
- 2 cups or bowls
- 48 small items (stones, beans, seeds, or buttons)

Object of the Game:
Capture more seeds than your opponent in your mancala bowl.

Before You Begin:
1. Place four items, called seeds, in each of the twelve sections, called holes, of the egg carton. The egg carton is the game board.
2. Place a bowl on each side of the game board. This is your mancala bowl.
3. Set the game board horizontally between you and your opponent.
4. Each player's mancala board is the side of the carton closest to him or her.

Rules of Play:

1. You can only move seeds on your side of the game board (the bottom row).

2. On your turn, pick up all the seeds from one hole on your side of the board. Moving counter-clockwise around the whole board, place one seed in each hole. Your mancala bowl counts as a hole on your turn but skip your opponent's mancala bowl.

3. If the last seed on your turn lands in your mancala bowl, you get another turn.

4. If the last seed on your turn lands in an empty hole on your side of the game board then you capture that seed and all the seeds directly across from it. All captured pieces go to your mancala bowl.

5. The game ends when all six holes on one player's side are empty. Any seeds left on a side are added to that player's mancala bowl.

6. Count all the seeds in each mancala bowl. The player with the most seeds wins.

RECIPE: PEANUT BUTTER STEW

Peanuts are a common ingredient in many African recipes. They're a popular and important source of protein throughout most of the continent. Enjoy this peanut butter stew.

Ingredients:

2 tablespoons (30 milliliters) oil (peanut, vegetable, or olive)

1 large onion, finely chopped

2 pounds (900 grams) meat (chicken, beef, or lamb), cut into 1½ inch (3-4 centimeter) pieces

1-2 sweet potatoes, cut into ½ inch (1-2 centimeters) pieces

½ cup (125 grams) peanut butter

1½ cups (350 milliliters) cold water

⅓ cup (75 grams) tomato paste

2 cups (475 milliliters) hot water

4 carrots, cut into ½ inch (1-2 centimeters) pieces

2 teaspoons (10 milliliters) dried thyme

2 bay leaves

salt and pepper, to taste

Directions:

Heat the oil in a large saucepan and add the minced onion. Cook over medium heat until the onion is translucent, stirring occasionally. Add the meat to the saucepan. Cook the meat until lightly browned, stirring as needed. Then, add the carrots and sweet potatoes.

In a bowl, mix the peanut butter with the cold water and stir. Pour the mixture in the saucepan, over the meat and vegetables. Add the tomato paste and hot water to the stew, stirring well to mix all ingredients.

Add the thyme, salt, pepper, and bay leaves. Cover and cook on low heat for one to two hours. Stir the stew occasionally.

Remove the bay leaves prior to serving.

Serve over white rice.

GLOSSARY

archeologists (ahr-kee-OL-uh-jists): a person who studies the distant past and often digs up old buildings, objects, and bones to examine them carefully

colonies (KAH-luh-neez): territories that have been settled by people from another country and are controlled by that country

dormant (DOR-muhnt): a dormant volcano is not doing anything now but could erupt again

enslaved (in-SLAYVED): to make a slave of

industry (IN-duh-stree): manufacturing companies and other businesses

mosaic (moh-ZAY-ic): a pattern or picture made up of small pieces of colored stone, tile, or glass

natural resources (NACH-ur-uhl REE-sors-iz): materials produced by the Earth that are necessary or useful to people

primates (PRYE-mates): any members of the group of mammals that includes monkeys, apes, and humans

rural (ROOR-uhl): of or having to do with the countryside, country life, or farming

safari (suh-FAHR-ee): a trip taken, especially in Africa, to see or hunt large wild animals

urban (UR-buhn): having to do with or living in a city

INDEX

SHOW WHAT YOU KNOW

1. What kinds of land are in Africa?

2. Why does Africa have so many plants and animals?

3. Name three ways Europeans used Africa to make money.

4. What are some health concerns in Africa?

5. How are African children like you?

FURTHER READING

Edinger, Monica, *Africa is My Home: A Child of the Amistad*, Candlewick, 2015.

Koontz, Robin, *Learning About Africa*, Lerner Publications, 2015.

Erskine, Kathryn, *Mama Africa!: How Miriam Makeba Spread Hope with Her Song*, Farrar, Straus and Giroux, 2017.

ABOUT THE AUTHOR

Annette Whipple is a children's nonfiction author living in southeastern Pennsylvania with her husband and three children. She strives to inspire a sense of wonder in young people while exciting them about science, social studies, and writing. When she's not writing, Annette enjoys reading a good book and snacking on warm chocolate chip cookies. Learn more about Annette, her books, and her presentations at *www.AnnetteWhipple.com*.

Meet the Author!
www.meetREMauthors.com

www.rourkeeducationalmedia.com

PHOTO CREDITS: Cover and p1: ©Ali Ender Birer, ©evenfh, ©uchar, ©chuvipro, ©Fabian Plock, ©Craig Dingle, p4: ©NosUA, p5: ©kosmozoo, p6: ©boezie, p7: ©Bartosz Hadyniak, ©yoh4nn, p8: ©Byrdyak, ©Phototreat, p9: ©demarfa, ©Friedemeier, p10: ©Gleb_Ivanov, p11: ©USO, ©nikpal, p12: ©Piotr Krze?lak, ©mtcurado, ©JohnCarnemolla, ©rhardholt, p13: ©Holger Mette, p14: ©Wiki, ©Fabian Plock, p15: ©Grafissimo, p16: ©duncan1890, p17: World History Archive / Alamy Stock Photo, p18: ©Wiki, p19: ©RichSTOCK / Alamy Stock Photo, ©Tempura, p20: ©MShep2, ©helovi, p21: ©hadynyah, p:22: ©HomoCosmicos, p23: ©Jacek_Sopotnicki, ©By Joseph Sohm, p24: ©THEGIFT777, ©mariusFM77, p25: ©InnaFelker, p26: ©Kenneth Sponsler, p28: ©Paul Brighton, p29: ©Natikka

Edited by: Keli Sipperley
Cover and Interior design by: Rhea Magaro-Wallace

Library of Congress PCN Data

Africa / Annette Whipple
 (Earth's Continents)
  ISBN 978-1-64156-407-6 (hard cover)
  ISBN 978-1-64156-533-2 (soft cover)
  ISBN 978-1-64156-657-5 (e-Book)
Library of Congress Control Number: 2018930428

Rourke Educational Media
Printed in the United States of America,
North Mankato, Minnesota

HO